all Around the Circle

Written by **CARA KANSALA**

Art by **CARA KANSALA & MAX DOREY**

Uncle Brooklyn

Uncle Brooklyn's in a pickle,
Pearl the cat's across the tickle.
She didn't swim, on this he'd bet,
'Cause Pearl the cat hates getting wet.
She didn't row there in a dory,
That would be a foolish story.
Pearl the cat, she could not fly
So how she'd get there, by and by?
She did not wade or skip or float
Or sail there in a sailing boat.
She could have hitched a ride with Joe
When he went jigging, rowing slow,
But Joe he can't stand cats, you see,
Because old Joe has allergies.
Aunt Maud's cat Pearl, so far from home,
Across the tickle she did roam.
But how'd she cross the water wide?
She could have done it at low tide,
But Pearl's wee paws,
they would be soaking,
Possibly, she would be choking.
Now she sleeps upon the rocks
Underneath the harbour docks.
So Uncle Brooklyn looked some more
And stared until his eyes were sore.
The cat he saw had one black paw
And wasn't Pearl the cat at all!

Nan and Poppies

Nan, she loved poppies, and Poppy loved Nan
So he planted them when they first wed.
Nan, she loved Poppy and planted the seeds
In her garden to keep her love fed.

He worked on a trawler; she scrubbed all the floors.
He split all the wood and she scrubbed them some more.
He mended the nets and she knitted the socks.
She worked splitting fish and he worked on the docks.

And when they got older, he cared for her still.
He brought her the tea, let it cool on the sill.
He rubbed her old shoulders and brushed her grey hair.
He warmed up the broth and he fed her with care.

And when they got older, she cared for him still.
She put on his slippers and brought him his pills.
She rubbed his old fingers and smoothed out his hair.
She sang him old love songs, he rocked in his chair.

And now there is silence; the house it stands still.
The curtains have faded, there's dust on the sill.
But the flowers still bloom, and the poppies still stand
Because Nan, she loved poppies, and Poppy loved Nan.

Aunt Bun's Red Dress

Aunt Bun's red dress
Was a fancy frock from town.
It cost her more than three months wage
And Nanny, oh she frowned.

She wore that dress to every dance
And danced until the dawn,
And when the sun came up sometimes
She danced upon the lawn.

She wore that dress to Sunday lunch,
To bingo night and cards.
She wore that dress to feed the goats
And chased them in the yard.

She wore that dress to clean the fish
And salt it on the flakes.
She wore that dress to knead the dough,
To boil the jam and bake.

She wore that dress until she met
The apple of her eye,
And then she wore it to the church
And sauntered up the aisle.

She wore that dress each time she brought
Her babies home to stay.
To christenings, births and funerals,
She wore it every day.

She wore it 'til the day she died,
Aunt Bun was ninety-four.
And when she breathed her long last breath
It fell upon the floor.

Aunt Bun's red dress had served her well,
Its polka dots long gone,
And only it remembered how
She'd danced upon the lawn.

The Barn Door

Lukey's drawers hung on the line
But Lukey wasn't feeling fine
'Cause Lukey'd had to chase the goat
And fell into his Poppy's boat.
The boat it tipped and in the drink
Went Lukey, oh that boy could sink,

But Uncle Clar was there, thanks be,
And hauled him out and cursed the sea.
The boat it sank and Poppy cried
Then Lukey, boy, he told a lie,
"I don't know how the goat got out!
Unhinged the door without a doubt!

She ate a sock, then butted me
And then she kicked my poor left knee!"
"Sure, you're not limping!" Poppy bawled
So Lukey fell and limped and crawled.
"You clean forgot to close the door,
You silly boy, you've done it 'fore.
You silly boy, it's plain to see
You're limping with your good right knee!"

Isn't Life Quite Grand?

Scratchy Sour-Puss, Scratchy Sour-Puss padding up the lane

Da-Doodle Dum, Da-Doodle-Daw

He raps upon the pane

"Missus, can Old Itchy Dear come out and play today"

Da-Doodle Dum, Da-Doodle-Daw

There's hardly any rain

Old Itchy and young Scratchy slowly ramble to the docks

Da-Doodle Dum, Da-Doodle-Daw

They slumber on the rocks

Old Itchy tells young Scratchy that the world's a lovely place

Da-Doodle Dum, Da-Doodle-Daw

She's lived a life of grace

Young Scratchy helps Old Itchy home when dusk falls on the land

Da-Doodle Dum, Da-Doodle-Daw

Yes, isn't life quite grand?

While Uncle Jack Was Jigging

While Uncle Jack was jigging,
Aunt Mary baked a pie,
Old Tom Cat watched the capelin roll,
And Agnes hung the line.

While Uncle Jack was jigging,
The sheep grazed down the lane,
The salt meat boiled,
The ocean roiled,
The chicks pecked at the grain.

While Uncle Jack was jigging,
Old Bertha mended vamps,
The crows came calling two-by-two,
And Poppy trimmed the lamps.

While Uncle Jack was jigging,
The table it was laid,
Nan put out her best blue vase,
And cousin Tommy played.

While Uncle Jack was jigging,
Old Pete chewed on his bone,
And Doris paced about the house
Until her Jack came home.

The Worried Chicken

Heloise the chicken
always worried 'bout the rain,
'Bout thunderstorms and creaky doors,
'Bout

FaLLinG

in the grain...

'Bout winter chills and bucket spills,

About the night and day,

'Bout allergies and too much sun,

'Bout sneezing in the hay.

She worried if the rooster

COCKADOODLEDOOD too loud,

She worried while she slept

And also worried in a crowd.

She worried that her feathers weren't as white as they could be,

'Bout ticks and lice and mice and ants,

And bugs and snakes and fleas.

She worried that she worried not enough and too much too.

She worried that the sky was sometimes not the brightest blue.

She worried that a ladybird might land upon her feathers

And that it might decide to stay in any kind of weather.

So tiny was the ladybird that landed on the chicken,

And if she knew, oh Heloise, she surely would be stricken.

The tiny bug, she slept with not a worry, click or clue,

And Heloise the chicken started worrying 'nough for two.

Here Comes the Sun

While weary clouds gathered,
Hearts weathered the storm.
And you softly sang,
Here comes
The sun.

With hearts still in tatters
And eyes newly born,
The sun, you sang,
Here, love,
It comes.

With tip-toeing fingers,
Your hand reached for mine.
The sun, you sang,
Look, love,
It's near.

With tears falling slowly,
I gave you my heart.
The sun, you sang,
Look, love,
It's here.

Charlotte and Pip

Charlotte, each morning, sets off on a trip
She skips to the tickle to see her friend Pip
Ticky-boo. Ticky-La. ticky-day-diddle-doe
Ticky-boo. ticky-la. ticky-day

Pip, every morning, she smiles when she sees
Her dearest friend Charlotte kick up her goat knees
Ticky-boo. Ticky-La. ticky-day-diddle-doe
Ticky-boo. ticky-la. ticky-day

They dance in the sweetness of dawn's early rays
They dance and they jig while the water makes waves
Ticky-boo. Ticky-La. ticky-day-diddle-doe
Ticky-boo. ticky-la. ticky-day

Charlotte is older and teaches Pip tricks
Waltzes and tangos and limbos with sticks
Ticky-boo. Ticky-La. ticky-day-diddle-doe
Ticky-boo. ticky-la. ticky-day

They dine on the sweet grass and nap under tress
Then chat with the chickens and buzz with the bees
Ticky-boo. Ticky-La. ticky-day-diddle-doe
Ticky-boo. ticky-la. ticky-day

And when the sun's setting wee Pip says good night
And Charlotte skips back up the lane out of sight
Ticky-boo. Ticky-La. ticky-day-diddle-doe
Ticky-boo. ticky-la. ticky-day

And both of them sing to the stars in the sky
Then sleep while the moon dances, rising up high
Ticky-boo. Ticky-La. ticky-day-diddle-doe
Ticky-boo. ticky-la. ticky-day

On Tuesday Morning We Fed the Goat

On Tuesday morning we fed the goat,
At supper it fed us,
But lean and lousy was the roast,
No meat was on old Gus.

So Nan, she made a stew of cod
That Pop fetched from the store,
But Ann had left the cover off
And Nan was wicked sore.

So Nan, she baked a three-bun loaf
And cooled it on the sill.
The wind came up and knocked it down
And Nan was wicked ill.

So Nan, she tried to make a meal
With fresh trout from the pond,
But Hazel slipped and dropped the fish.
Poor Nan, she was beyond.

So Nan, she thought she'd bake a cake
With berries picked by Dad,
But Ambrose tripped and spilled them all.
Oh Nan, she was so mad.

And so it went that Nan,
She never cooked another roast.
She fed the goats and milked them too
And sometimes we ate toast.

Because poor Nan remembered well
And Nan, she knew he'd gloat,
The toughest, meanest, leanest buck,
Old Gus, the Tuesday Goat.

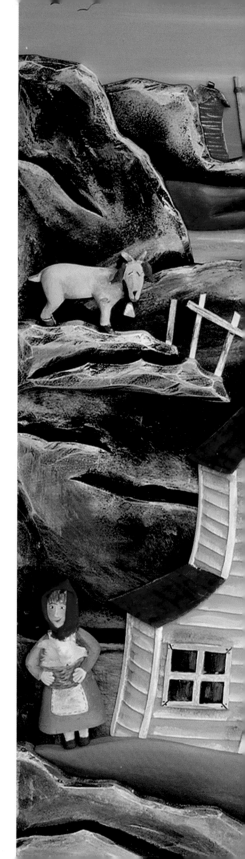

The House Next Door

Up the road I used to go
To Gull Rock on the hill.
While lilacs grew and breezes blew,
The time stood silent still.

For years I walked upon this road
And stood upon this land,
And for a time I too stood still
For years I couldn't stand.

There used to be an ochre house
Built on the hill above
With yellow glass and tarnished brass,
A house once filled with love.

A house once filled with love,
My Love, it hurts to be alone.
I turn my back and walk away,
My heart is now my own.

The
Petty Harbour Cow

There was a cow that couldn't moo,

But she could sing and sneeze ATCHOO!

She couldn't moo, but she could burp

And cackle, buzz, and gasp and slurp.

She couldn't moo but she could jabber,

Mumble, murmur, shriek and blabber,

Sigh and slobber, sniff and snore,

She'd take a nap then snore some more!

Sigh and weep and whine and whimper,

whisper, mutter, munch and simper,

Laughed until her tum was sore

Then try to moo and laughed some more.

She'd try to "moo" but only "meed"

And then she'd laugh until she peed.

That Petty Harbour cow she tried

To moo until the day she died

And just before her timely death

She opened wide and took a breath

And **MOO**ed the loudest moo she could

And smiled and thought that life was good.

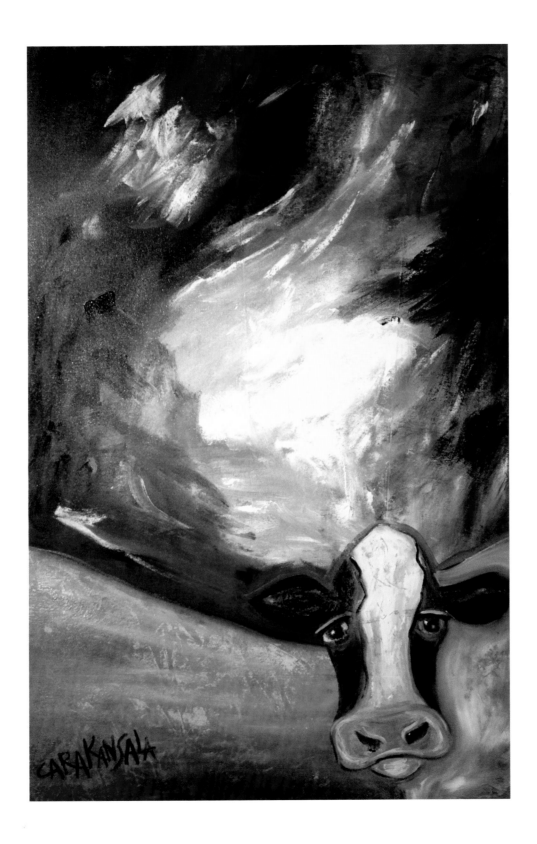

Itchy's Moonsong

On autumn nights at summer's edge,
Sweet Itchy'd watch the stars.
She'd search for moonbeams, listening close
For nightsongs from afar.

On her whiskers, dragonflies
Would waltz and play their tunes
And like a harp they'd pluck her strings
While Itchy swayed and swooned.

And in her dreams the poppies bloomed
And turned forever red,
And Itchy'd cuddle in their warmth
A cuddly, poppy bed.

She'd dream of friends she'd loved and lost,
She'd dream of loves that stayed
And sing her moonsongs while she purred
Until the dawn of day.

The Dance

For so many moons he loved her
And they danced upon the stage
Where once he'd been a red-faced boy,
Where they had been engaged.

They jigged and waltzed through seas of tears,
They tangoed in the rain,
They polka-ed through the toughest times,
And tip-toed through the pain.

He'd found a way to find some joy
In times that could be rough.
She'd found a way to ease her heart
When things were feeling tough.

And through the years they'd grown as one
You'd notice in a glance,
The way they moved with hearts so full,
The beauty of the dance.

Lolly Lundrigan's Tulips

Lolly Lundrigan liked to say
She'd been abroad, she'd lived "away."
She liked to show her fancy home
So stuffed with things she'd brought
from Rome,

The curtains she'd had made in Wales,
Her hand-dyed rugs and hand-carved rails,
Velvet tables found in France.
She'd sit at wearing Irish pants.

Embroidered towels from Budapest
She'd dry off with then sit and rest
On pillows from the Great White North
With cuckoo clocking back and forth.
Poor Lolly thought the world it cared

'Bout what she had and what she'd wear,
But Uncle Dobbin's goats cared not
About the shrubs and trees she'd bought.
They munched away then bleated twice,
"Imported tulips taste quite nice."

Marc Chagull

Bonjour! cried Marc, as he rode by,
The dashing gull from France,
Who painted paintings all day long,
Wore "pantaloons," not pants.
He often had a basket full of baguettes, figs, and Brie
And sometimes I would smile at him
And he would wink at me.

He brought his brushes everywhere
And painted often in "plein aire."
He painted dreamy skies and seas
With goats proposing on their knees.
He painted moons that danced in nights
That kissed the stars and twinkled bright.

Au Revoir! cried Marc, as he rode by,
The handsome gull from France,
Who painted paintings all day long,
Grew "plantes" et "fleurs," not plants.
He wore a tam cocked to one side
And on his neck a tie
And sometimes he would smile at me
As he went sailing by.

Midnight Dreamers

Watch the moon, just look, my love,
And you might see it smile.
Pluck the stars like peaches ripe,
And keep them for a while

In pockets made for treasured stones
That shine like marbles bright.
Let your wishes flood the sky,
We'll button up the night.

We'll button up the night, my love,
And tuck it in with care.
We'll keep it in a quiet place
Until we need to share
Our midnight wish, our smiling moon
With friends who've lost their way
On roads where midnight dreamers walk
And softly wind songs say,

Come along with me, my love,
I'll hold you in my heart.
Come along, I'll hold you tight;
I've held you from the start.
Unbutton buttons far too tight,
You've found a place to stay.
Close your eyes and dream, my love,
You've finally found your way.

**For my Grandmother, Beatrice Coles,
Also known as "Nanabanana."**

Thank you for your hugs and encouragement, for raking leaves
and sweeping the front steps in your brazier when you were hot,
and for teaching me to always be real.

A CIP catalogue record for this book is available from Library and Archives Canada.

Text ©2017 Cara Kansala and Art ©2017 Cara Kansala & Max Dorey

www.breakwaterbooks.com

Paperback 978-1-55081-675-4

Breakwater Books is committed to choosing papers and materials for our
books that help to protect our environment. To this end, this book is printed on a
recycled paper that is certified by the Forest Stewardship Council®

Printed in Canada